JOSH
and the
WooWoo

David Bedford
Daniel Howarth

QED
QED Publishing

Josh didn't like noise. The problem was...

Josh had five very NOISY brothers...
and six EVEN NOISIER sisters!

Josh tried going outside, but it wasn't any better.

BOOM-BOOM! Clang-a-lang-a-lang!

Wherever they were and whatever they did,
Josh's brothers and sisters made as much
noise as a herd of elephants.

"Let's play in the woods!" shouted his brothers.

Josh's brothers and sisters thumped
down to the bottom of the garden,
leaving Josh behind.

"Good!" said Josh. And for the first time all day, he uncovered his big, flip-floppy ears.

Josh was just about to play quietly in the sandpit, when...

Josh hid under a bucket, feeling all shivery-shaky until the HORRIBLE noise went away.

Josh's brothers came racing back.
"Nobody's scared of a HELICOPTER!"
they laughed. But Josh WAS!

"Come with us," said his brothers.
"We'll look after you."

Josh's brothers **bounced** noisily over the garden gate...

into the meadow, leaving Josh behind again.

"Good!" said Josh, uncovering his ears.

He was just about to play quietly with a flittery-fluttery butterfly, when...

CHUGGA-CHUGGA-CHUGGA-CHUGGA!

Josh hid behind his ears,
feeling all wibbly-wobbly until
the TERRIBLE noise went away.

Josh's sisters came skipping back.
"Nobody's scared of a TRACTOR!"
they giggled. But Josh WAS!

"Come with us," said his sisters.
"We'll look after you."

Josh's sisters wriggled noisily
through the hedge, leaving
Josh behind again.

"Good!" said Josh, as his brothers and sisters thundered into the woods, making the ground shake.

He was just watching a flippety-flappety bird fly by, when...

Ssssss! Puff! Puff!

Josh's brothers and sisters came bounding towards him. "HIDE!" they shouted. "Something's coming!"

"What is it?" asked Josh, curiously.
The noise was very quiet.

"WE DON'T KNOW!" they yelled.

They were scared, but Josh WASN'T!

What could it be? Josh thought. He crept
up the hill to find out.

chuffa-chuffa

The noise slowly became louder.

chuffa-chuffa, **CHUFFA-CHUFFA**
CLICKETY-CLACK, **CLICKETY-CLACK**

WOOOO! WOOOOOOOO!

It was louder than anything he had ever heard, but it wasn't HORRIBLE or TERRIBLE. It made Josh tingle from his ears to his toes!

Chuffa-chuffa went the chimney.
Clickety-clack went the wheels on the track.

WOOO! WOOO! went the whistle
as the bright-red steam engine thundered past.

From then on, Josh was never left behind
when there was a hissing, puffing....

WOOOO!
WOOOO!

Notes for parents and teachers

- Before you read this book to a child, or children, look at the front cover and ask what they think the story is about.

- Read the story to the children and then ask them to read it to you, helping them with unfamiliar words and praising them for their efforts.

- Which is the children's favourite picture in the book? Discuss with them why they particularly like it.

- Ask the children to close their eyes and listen for a moment or two. What sounds can they hear? Josh was frightened of some noises. Are there any noises the children are frightened of? What about helicopters and police cars?

- Discuss with the children what it feels like when they are scared. Can they think of ways to make themselves feel better?

- Do the children think Josh was brave to go and find out what was making the strange chuffa-chuffa noise? Talk about what it means to be brave. Can the children think of a time when they were brave? Ask them to talk about it.

- Discuss with the children why Josh liked the steam train so much. In what way are steam trains different from other trains?

- Have any of the children ever seen or been for a ride on a steam train?

- Have the children seen rabbits in the wild? Do they know where rabbits live and what they eat?

- Ask the children to draw a picture of Josh helping to drive the steam engine. Show them the illustration in the book if they need help with it. Use paints, crayons or coloured pencils to make it more colourful.

Copyright © QED Publishing 2009

First published in the UK in 2009 by
QED Publishing
A Quarto Group Company
226 City Road
London EC1V 2TT

www.qed-publishing.co.uk

ISBN 978 1 84835 240 7

Printed in China

Author David Bedford
Illustrator Daniel Howarth
Designer Alix Wood
Project Editor Heather Amery